The Twins

Alice Veis

Contents

Chapter 1

Natalie's POV

Her outfit

" Now Rain, River be good don't give your nanny a headache" I said kissing my children forehead

" ok mommy " they said in unison before running off to play

I smiled at them before waving at the nanny and set off to work

As much as I might hate this job I need it to take care of my kids because I have no clue as to where there father is

One month after the best sex ever, well first time ever having sex I found out I was pregnant and when I told my parents they told me to pack up and leave

Through out my pregnancy I worked at stores earning enough money to get off the street and after they where born I got a job at the strip club

It's been 6 years now and I'm still in working there

I didn't attend university so I didn't really have anything to get a real job

Finally I arrived at my destination and parked in the lot grabbing my work bag along with my stripper heels

I walked into the dressing room where the others dancers where getting ready

" Ladies show starts in 10 minutes, OH Natalie your performing alone tonight so your up right before the girls you have 5 minutes" My boss Ethan said

I quickly stripped from my clothes and got dressed in the outfit I would be wearing

I slipped my heels on and quickly let my hair out

" Let's welcome your favourite dancer VIXEN" I heard Ethan yell, and I took that as my que to walk out

" Now or never" I muttered and started my routine

Her outfit

Demon's POV

" dude come on you gotta get out tonight " My bestfriend Keith said and Edwin agreed

" yea bro, you need to go out have a drink, we're going to BLACKMAGIC strip club, I hear they have the best strippers " Edwin said

" fine" I said as it came out harsher than expected

I stood up and fixed my suit and we left my office

We didn't wait in line as they knew who I was, we went into the VIP area and sat with drinks in our hands

" Let's welcome your favourite dancer VIXEN" I heard Ethan said and a blonde hair girl walked out her head down as whistles and howling where heard

I sat back in my seat sipping my Henessy as she started to dance

As she danced and stared at her

She looked oddly familiar

The way she bent and danced almost got me hard

I looked at her longer and realisation hit me

The damn girl I have be looking for 6 years

The girl that 20 year old me fell in love with that faithful night January 15

As if she sensed me looking at her gorgeous face she looked up at me and a mixture of emotions flashed through her eyes

She almost messed up but caught herself and turning it into a split

Soon she was done and she quickly grabbed the robe she out with and walked to the backstage

Natalie POV

I rushed off the stage and went to the dressing room

" great performing as always" Ethan said handing 2 bags of cash

" got to do, what you have to do" I said taking the bag and when he left I changed into something less sweety and hot

Natalie's outfit

I packed up everything and left to thr parking lot

I unlocked my truck dropping my bags in then closing it

I went to unlock my door before a large tattooed hand closed it back

I felt breathing on my neck and I knew who it was

" where have you been hiding " he said, his voice coming out deep and smelled like weed

" nowhere" I said calmly as possible

" is that so, do you know who I am?" He said fiddling with my hair my back still turned towards his chest

I shook my head lieing as he chuckled

" Yes,do remember that night 6 years ago at this same exact club" he said as memories flashed before my eyes

Before I could respond my phone rang, when I looked down I saw that it was a facetime from the kids nanny

Not caring that he was right behide me, I answered

" oh thank god you answered, Rain fell down the stairs and hit her head we are the hospital right downtown" she said holding a crying River

I started to panic searching for my keys

" I want my mommy" I heard River cry

" can you fucking move" I said pushing him away

" mommy is on the way baby" I said starting my car and drove away leaving a confused father that knew nothing about his children

I arrived to the hospital and ran inside

" Hi Rain Thomas " I said

" room 239" she said and I ran down the hall

" how is she" I said picking up River

" the doctors said she's resting and to give them a while" she said exhausted

" thank you so much Crystal you should go home and rest" I said paying her extra and she left

I walked outside still holding River his head resting on my shoulder

I walked up to my car and right as I was about to open my door I heard a voice

" Natalie" from that voice

Chapter 2

Natalie's POV

"Natalie" I heard his voice

" what" I said wiping the stray tears from my sons face

" I need you to come with me and you can give the kids to there rightful father" he said sticking his tattooed hand in his pocket

" OH give me children to the rightful father, okay then here take him cause your the rightful father" I said finally turning around to face him

" oh and yes there's a second one, she is sitting inside that hospital more than likely in pain getting medication because she fell off a stairs and hit her head, so yes sure go ahead and take them cause they are your children" I said opening my back door and getting a blanket throwing over River

He was too stunned to speak

I walked back inside the hospital and noticed he was following me

I went to Rain's room and he still followed me

I sat in the chair next to her bed and held River next to her covering them both and laid my head beside her head holding her hand and she held it

It brought back so much memories, the day they entered this world and they held my pinky for the first time ever

"mommy my head hurts" she said

" it's fine baby, I'm sure the medicine will work soon" I said rubbing her head

" medicine disgusting,I feel bad for you Rain" River said making a disgusted face

"who's the scary guy mommy" Rain said

" I will-" I was cut off by there father

" I'm your father, and you guys and your mom are gonna come live with me" he said

They got excited and I excused myself and told him to follow me

" you know you can't just barge into there lives like that" I said crossing my arms

" they are my kids that I put in you" he said angrily

" I don't even know your name, you probably don't even know my fucking name and you want us living with you" I said getting upset

" it's Demon now you know and your name is Natalie and I certainly don't give 3 fucks if you refuse cause you don't have a choice, what are there names?"

"Rain is the girl and River is the boy" I said

" I'm sure Rain and River would like a fresh start and I don't want to be a deadbeat father so I want to start taking care of both and my kids" he said

" you already look like a deadbeat dad" I muttered

He grabbed my jaw tightly making me look up at him

" how was I suppose to be a good father if I didn't know she about them " he said

I was mad that I didn't know what to say

He let me go when he saw a nurse coming

" are you Miss Thomas?" She asked

"yea that's me"

" well Rain is doing good, she can leave tomorrow just make sure she gets rest" she said handing me a discharge sheet

I said thanks and went back into the room

I filled it out and got Rain dressed in her Pj's

"Mommy Up" Rain said

" me too" River said and Demon watched to see what I would do

" better be lucky mommy got strong knees and can still bend cause she getting old" I said picking them up and spinning around with them

" mommy your only 25" They said laughing making Demon chuckle

I smiled at my gorgeous creations and kissed them

"let's get you guys home" I said

"I want dad to hold me now" Rain said

He looked at me for confirmation and I nodded handing her over

He held her on his hip carefully as if she was fragile

We walked to the front desk and I handed in the form and they gave me a prescription for pain medication for kids

We got home in 40 minutes and Demon followed my car the whole time

here house

I parked in my drive way and he parked his black tinted Bentley on the side walk

When he stepped out my neighbour Vanessa came out and came over bearly wearing anything

" mommy the witch is stepping on our lawn" River said making Rain laugh and they ran inside

I sighed closing my door when she stood infront of me

" hey Nat, mind setting me up with your sexy friend here" she said pushing her large breast up

" don't need my kids father getting whatever STD your carrying" I said and she scowled at me

" always being a bitch" she said pointing her finger in my face

" always being a whore" I said pointing my finger back in her face

She came up way too much in my face and was about to slap me when I slapped her across her face first making her head move to fast swiftly

" oh, you want to fight" she said catching her wig up

" it's too late for your bullshit Vanessa " I said

"scared"

" Never, walk away bitch before I turn you inside out " I said grabbing her by her shirt

" Next time I will get you" she said as I shoved her away

" Yea and the next time you set your ugly scarecrow looking ass on this motherfucking lawn I will kill you" I said

"Are you threatening me" she said

" no, its a promise " I said as she walked away off my lawn

"Fucking slut" I muttered

- "What a good show, fighting over me already" Demon said smirking

"don't flatter yourself" I said walking inside

He stayed a little bit before it was time for him to go

" Pack you all stuff up, I will be here 10 am sharp tomorrow and I am very impatient" he said before kissing the kid's forehead and he left

I locked up and went to tuck the kids in bed

I turned their bedroom light off and went to my room

I showered and changed into my Pj's and crawled into my bed falling asleep in no time

Chapter 3

Natalie's POV

I woke up remembering what today is

I rolled out of my bed pulling my sleeping my shorts down

I looked at my phone seeing that it was 9:58, I rolled my eyes not caring that Demon was going to be here soon

I left the kids to sleep and played my Queen Naija playlist as I packed up stuff around my house

10 am soon came around and I woke the kids up, and Demon was right on time

"Daddy" the kids said excitedly

Great already replacing me

"heyy" he said picking them both up

"I thought I said get ready by 10" he said glaring at me

"mommy just woke us up she was cleaning" Rain said wiggling down "alright go brush your teeth and I will make you guys some breakfast" I said shooing them away

I sighed and finished packing the rest of the stuff up and tapping boxes

"Mommy where done" River said dragging Rain behind him

"smile for mommy and lemme smell"

they smiled and let me smell there mouth

"good job" I said holding there hands to the kitchen

Demon followed and I put them on the bar stools

I took two bowls out and grabbed 3 vanilla yogurts and 3 strawberry yogurts

I poured them in the bowls and then took kiwi's, strawberries and banana's slicing them up and putting them in the bowls

I then added oats and granola in the bowls and gave them there spoons

I got there cups out and poured orange juice in there cups handing it to them, the left them to eat

"good see that the mother of my children actually cares for my kids"

" did you take me for a bum ass mom cause I'm a stripper"

"could say that" he said snickering

" well for your information, I had to more from my parents house cause they didn't have space or money and I had to do a shit ton of jobs while pregnant, went into labor at work and then had to get a job at the strip club as a stripper to care for my children to make sure they are healthy, and everything is up to standard" I said upset before walking off

I picked put our outfits and fixed my hair and did a little bit of makeup

Natalie and kids outfit

The house

The living room

The Kitchen

Kid's room, closet and bathroom

Natalie and Demon's room, closet and bathroom

" This is nice" I said

" yep, designed it myself" he said

" lets me show you guys your room" he said picking them up and walking up the stairs and I followed

when we got in the room I was awe strucked

" oh my god, mommy look its beautiful" River said

" mommy see's baby" I said

Demon came to stand beside me as we watched our children play

" where sharing a room, just so you know" he said with the same unemotional looking face and his arm crossed across his chest

" why?" I said

" because I said so" he said walking away

" mommy where hungry?" they said in unison

" lets go see what your dad has in his kitchen" I said picking up Rain and holding River's hand

we got lost a few times but soon found it

I made steak, seasoned asparigous and mask potato with some sauce

what she made

I made my kids plate first giving them fruit punch in cups and gave them there forks

Demon came down a few minutes later in black sweatpants and he was shirtless

I averted my eyes away from him and gave him a plate

" thanks" he said and soon started to eat

I made myself a plate and drank water

when everyone was done I cleaned up the kitchen and I gave them a bath and got them dressed in there pjs

well more like I gave Rain a bath and River shoved me out

I tucked them in and read them a bible story and kissed there foreheads

" mommy loves you my babies" I said

Demon came in and kissed there foreheads

" love you daddy" they said sleepy

" love you too" he muttered

we left the room and I took out some sleep shorts and top and went into the shower

I got dressed and placed my hair in a messy-bun and nervously got in the bed

I got under the covers and cuddled into the pillow

" good night sweet cheeks"

" good night " I muttered

Here goes nothing

Chapter 4

N atalie's POVDay 3

Natalie and the kids outfit

I got up early this morning and the bed was empty like it was on the first and second day

I sighed and got started with my day which was cleaning the room and waking the kids up

I strolled to there bedroom and opened there bedroom doors and they where fast asleep

I walked over to there curtains and opened them and they groaned

" Come in time to get up" I said

" Mommy but we don't even go to school anymore" Rain complained

If you are wondering why there not going anymore is because Demon refuses to send them and wants to homeschool them so a teacher comes over the house and tooters them and I must admit they are more advanced than they where before

They got up anyways and brushed there teeth before we headed downstairs

I started on breakfast which was a croissant breakfast sandwich and breakfast potatoes

I poured there mango peach juice in there cups and in mine before giving them there plates

There food

" Thank you mommy" they said in unison

" Where is daddy mommy" River asked

" I don't know baby" I said

" I'm right here" a deep voice said scaring me

I turned to see Demon in his normal work attire a black suit

" DADDY" the twins yelled and forgot all about there food running towards him

He picked them both up without a struggle and kissed there foreheads

He was so gentle with them but when it was me he was rough

I averted my attention from them and started to clean up leaving the twins food so they could finish it

I wiped the counters and stove down and packed whatever dish was there in the dishwasher

" Good morning " a voice said behide me

" Good morning" I replied not paying them much attention

" River and Rain finish up your food loves" I said and they nodded continuing to eat

Once they where done they threw whatever was left and I placed them in the dishwasher

They cleaned up after themselves and got there Notebooks and pencils ready for when there tooter would arrive

" Why are so quiet this morning"

" Well your not here every morning so I have no clue how you would know weather I have been quiet in the mornings for the past few days" I said washing my hands and throwing the kitchen towel down in the counter

" Who are you catching an attitude with "

" I'm sure your not blind because your the only person in here with me " I said

He wakes briskly to where I stood and grabbed me by my neck

He lowered his mouth to my ears and gus breath tickled me

" If I where you I would watch that pretty mouth before I fuck the shit out your pussy " he said lowly so I could here

I crossed my legs as my vagina throbbed

Gosh why does he still give me goosebumps after 6 years

He pulled away and fixed his jacket and just in time the tooter walked in

" Good morning Mr and Mrs Mendez" Lily said

" Oh lily where not-"

" Good morning Lily " Demon said cutting me off

She smiled at us before going to find the twins to begin there daily lessons

" Where legally changing the twins name to Mendez" he said before walking out to where the twins where

" Daddy when will you be back" I heard River ask

" I will be back before you know it" he said to them giving them a small smile and kissed there foreheads

He came back to the kitchen where I was and backed me up in the counter

I looked down not wanting to look into his tempting eyes before he lifted my chin and made me look at him

He pecked my lips twice surprising me

Gosh they where soft

" I will be back soon my love, when I come home I would like a little surprise" he said

" Preferably you in my bed naked and ready for daddy" he said kissing me again and this time I actually kissed back

God I'm horny

He smirked at me before walking out with his keys

Godddddd

I leaned on the counter and rubbed my face

He's gonna kill me, lord have mercy on me

I sighed and continued with my daily cleaning as the twins continued there lesson

I hope Demon was joking

I really Hope so

Chapter 5

Natalie's POV 8pm

The kids outfit

Natalie's outfit

" Alright and that's the end" I said closing the bible story book of Ruth and Naomi

" I like that story" Rain said yawning

" I do too" I said kissing both their lips

" Mommy when is daddy coming home"

" I don't know sweetie"

" Don't you have his number or something" River asked

" No love"

" Mommy I don't want to sound mean or anything but that's kind of stupid not to have his number"

" He is right" a familiar voice said

" True"

" Good night my loves" he said sitting on the bed edge and kissing both their cheeks

I packed the book away and turned there bedroom lights off leaving their nightlight on

I yawned tiredly and went into the room and got in the bed

It dipped and I suppose it was Demon

" What's your number" he said

I held my hand out and he dropped his phone in my hand and I typed in my number saving it as Natalie

I gave it back to him and got ready to fall asleep again

" What's your Instagram"

" Do you even use Instagram" I asked

" I do, so type yours in" he said calmly

I sighed and searched for myself under the name Natalie Thomas

@ NataliaThomas

Twins loading September 6,2017

@NatalieThomas

October 5, 2017Any day now River and Rain

@NatalieThomas

6 weeks progress

@NatalieThomas

My little loves, so proud to be your mommy

" Don't spam my shit" I muttered

I followed his page back just to see that had millions of followers and was only following 5 people including myself and posted only one photo of himself

I powered my phone off and closed my eyes hoping to fall asleep as quickly as possible and I did, thankfully

I was up to have any conversation tonight at all

The Next Day

I woke up early this morning and was going to start breakfast but the kitchen was empty

I had no clue where the hell a supermarket is around here but that's why I got a gps

I got dressed and went to to the kids room

They where already up and about

" Where going to the store babies get dressed" I said

" Can we match with you mommy" River asked and I smiled before nodding

I got there outfits out and got them dressed fixing their outfits

Natalie's and the kids outfit

I went downstairs and the kids ran to there father

" You guys look good where you off to"

" Mommy going to the store to get food for the house" Rain said and hummed in response

" Here's my card to buy the stuff" he said to me

" I don't need it" I said and he side eyed me before clearing his throat and standing up

" Go play kids" he said

He walked up to me and grabbed my neck making my breath hitch

" I was asking you love I was telling you" he said dropping it in my bag

He kissed my jawline and then pecked my lips before pulling away

I cleared my throat and averted my eyes and face from him as my cheeks where hot

" Kids let's go" I said taking my car keys up

He smirked at me before slapping my ass and he walked out lighting a cigar

I quickly buckled in the kids and got in the front seat

I set the gps up on my phone and a store was 5 minutes away

I drove up a large black gate where guards stood

This was surprising cause I have never been outside of the house for the past few days

What the hell does he do as a occupation

" Ma'am we can't let you out" the guy said sternly

A black Lamborghini pulled up and the tinted window rolled down

" Let them out" Demon said

" Yes boss" the security said and he sped pass driving out before me

I pulled off and drove down in a different direction and continued our journey to the store

I parked at got out holding both the kids hands as we crossed

I got a buggy and pushed it in the store looking from place to place to see what to get

I got shrimps, lobster, crab, drumsticks, wings

Then I got some veggies and fruits

I got snacks, yogurts, popsicles and chocolate and vanilla ones for me

I then got beer thinking about Demon as that was packed in the house

I got 6 bottles of juice and got 5 bottles of wine

Might as well spend money

I got wraps, rice and flour

Then moved on to the next isle to see what I should get

The kids dropped random stuff in the cart and I didn't pay them any attention

I then got juice boxes for the kids before moving along

I bounced into a guy and I said a quick sorry before walking away with the kids

I went into the cash register and cashed everything

In total I spend 400 dollars

I swiped his back card and it went through

She printed the receipt and they packed the stuff up in bags then in the buggy

" Remember to look before you cross my loves" I said as we crossed

I opened the trunk and packed the stuff in the back then put the trolly back

While getting into my car I saw the guy that I bounced get into his and I pulled out

The whole time he was driving behide me and when I pulled up to the gate he stopped

I drove in suspicious and he followed behide me

Demon was outside sitting down now wearing a grey sweatpants and a black t-shirt

He got up once he saw us and came towards the car

The other car stopped behide me

" Fucking weird" I muttered

A guy stepped out and he bro hugged Demon

" You didn't tell me you where stopping by Keith where's Edwin" Demon said

" Came to see my best friend, who's she" he said nodding towards me

" I will tell you later" Demon said taking the groceries out and held a sleeping River and I held Rain and my bag in my hand

I went inside and laid her on the couch and he laid River down before getting the other bags

I got started on dinner while Demon talked away with his friend in the other room

Demons POV

" So who is she" Keith asked

" Remember six years ago when I slept with a girl that I met at the strip club"

" Yea man you where obsessed and wouldn't stop searching for her even up until now"

" Well I found her and 6 years ago I got her pregnant and she had my kids that I had no clue was here but I secretly did a DNA test to make sure and it turns out those kids are mine" I explained

" Their ain't no doubt those kids aren't yours they look exactly like you " Keith said

" Yea I know just glad I found her she finally mine bro" I said

" And you look happy and you is happy , thank God you found her so you can stop rambling"

Soft footsteps where heard and it was Natalie

" Come on wake up it's time to eat" she said picking up the twins who groaned and laid on her shoulder

She was sure strong to pick those two heavy ass kids up

" Mommy few more minutes please" River said

He's just like me doesn't want to make up

" Well I'm hungry so" Rain said

" That's my girl" Natalie said

" You guys can come eat" she said to us before walking away with the kids

She made there plates and hers and we had to make ours

She gave them their cups which had mango juice in it and she drank wine

The food

" This is good mommy"

She smiled at our children and all you could see was love and I was glad that she genuinely loved our children

After all who wants a deadbeat baby mama cause imma put a next one in her real soon

Chapter 6

Natalie's POV 2weeks later

I looked in the full length mirror as I inspected my outfit

I was going to some ball that I forced to go to with Demon

Natalie's outfit

Demons outfit

" You look beautiful love" Demon said resting his hands in my hips

" But are we sure that this is save" he said moving the top of the dress exposing my top

I covered my breast and fixed the dress before clearing my throat

" It will be perfectly fine unless someone messes with it" I said spraying my rose perfume on

" Just making sure" he said holding his hand towards me

I held his hand and picked my bag up

We walked to our childrens room and they where fast asleep

I kissed both there forehead and smiled at them

" Mommy loves you guys" I said softly before walking out and Demon closed the door

We walked downstairs towards the nanny and I stopped

" We should be home no later than 12 " Demon said

" Make sure my children are safe" he said sternly and glared at her

She quickly nodded before saying

" Yes sir"

He intertwined our fingers and we went outside

The nanny closed the door behide us looking scared still

A black tinted limo was seen and he opened the door for me

He helped my in then got in as the driver locked the door

He pulled off and we sat in a awkward silence

I looked outside while he smoked his cigar and opened his legs wide

I sipped some wine as I knew my social battery was bound to run out and I needed to communicate as much as possible

The car came to a stop and we where at a expensive looking place

Paparazzi filled the place

Demon got out and flashes came his way

He held his hand out for me and I held it and got out

I looked down as flashes went off and we stopped at the carpet

Demons hands snaked around my waist and I smiled as they took different photos

He pulled me more towards him and my hand rested on his chest while his hands rested on my butt

" Brother" a voice said making us look towards the direction

" Tina" he said cracking a smile before it disappeared quickly

He pulled me along to the other side where his sister was taking photos with a guy

" Edwin" Demon said handshaking and bro hugging the guy

" I missed you so much " the girl said hugging him

" I missed you too Tina, how has mom and dad been" he asked

" They have been good they are here actually" Tina said

He quickly pulled me behide him and we went inside

We walked around until we stopped at a elderly couple

" Oh my god Demon" she exclaimed hugging him

" Hello mother" he said kissing her

This is so cute he really has a soft spot for people he loves

Can't say the same for myself

" Who is this beautiful young lady" she said standing and smiled at me and I smiled back

" I'm Natalia ma'am" I said

" Also my girlfriend and mother to your grandchildren" Demon said

Girlfriend!?

" Grandchildren" his mother said shocked

" Yes long story mother you will get to meet them tomorrow" he said

" Son look at you clean not a speck of dust a beautiful girl with you" his father said

" Always clean and yes a beautiful woman not girl" he said

They talked while I looked around and a arm grabbed me

Demons mother pulled me away so we could talk

" So how does my son have children to that I knew nothing about " she said

" Well we met six years ago and hooked up while drunk and I left in the morning before he woke up and I found out I was pregnant I knew nothing about him just how he looked, just a few weeks ago I was at work and he was somehow there and he followed me to the hospital because our daughter fell down some stairs at my house and we'll that's that's I guess "

" Oh dear did you go through your pregnancy all by yourself "

" I did my parents didn't approve and they forbade my sister for reaching out to me" I said

" Oh it's okay now dear you have his your family " she said and I smiled hugging her

She hugged me back patting my back

" Stealing my girlfriend now mother"

" Oh shut up and go kick rocks" she said rolling her eyes

I laughed softly and he glared at me

I looked away not wanting to feel like I was being scolded

Hours went by and I found out this party is a whole fucking gang and
business meeting

The father of my child is involved in this, it's not hard to believe but what
the hell

The drive home I was quiet and I got out of the limo leaving him

I went upstairs and showered then got dressed

I climbed into bed and got under the covers and thought about tomorrow

How would my kids react to all these new people

Only the lord knows

Chapter 7

Natalie's POV 5pm

Natalie and the kids outfits

I walked back in the house with the kids as we just came back from the park

" You ready to meet your grandparent's" I said to then and they nodded

We walked into the living room and Demon was there with his sister Tina and his parents who's names where Chrissy and Lorence

" Hey Natalie" Tina said smiling at me

" Hey Tina" I said smiling back

" Oh what beautiful children they look just like Demon, come here darlings I'm your grandma Chrissy" she said opening her arms to them

They ran and hugged her and she hugged them tight inhaling there smell and kissed them

" Oh god Lorence where gonna spoil them so much" she said and I chuckled

" Come sit" Tina said patting the space beside her

I sat down and she spoke

" So I'm planning to get pregnant but I wanted to here advice from someone who was once pregnant" she said

" Umm, at the first trimester it's like the worst honestly the second one is someone better and that trimester makes you wanna have more kids and the third the worst of them all you feel immense pain can hardly move around and your stomach drops so more pressure and weight" I said and she nodded

" But my best advice is to get a pregnancy pillow it safed my life and make sure to stay comfortable and know the foods to eat" I continued

" Thank you so much" she said and I nodded

" So how was your pregnancy " she asked

" It was hard, I was on my own for most of the time and had to work " I said

" Aww I'm sorry, so who looks after them like when you had to work"

" I had to hire someone couldn't trust my so call friends anymore because of a situation " I said and she nodded

" Would you have more kids" she asked

" Honestly I don't know maybe it's a mixed feeling right now " I said and she nodded

" I'm gonna get started on dinner" I said standing up

" Let me help you" Tina said and we headed to the kitchen

I was kinda making a handful of stuff and it would take a while

9pm

The food

" Everyone come eat" Tina called out

The kids dashed into the kitchen with everyone following close behide

I placed a portion of everything on the kids plate, mine, Demon's and his parents then Tina

I got 7 glasses down and poured juice in mine and the children's own and the others poured whatever they wanted in it

" This is really good girls" Chrissy said

" Thank you" I said and Tina nodded

" So where going on a vacation" Demon said breaking the silence putting his fork down

" To where son" Lorence said

" To Italy" he said and everyone got excited well except me but I smiled anyways to hide it

I finished eating and cleaned up the kitchen with the help of Chrissy and Tina

I went back to the bedroom and went to shower

I turned the shower on and while it heated up I stripped and then got in

" Natalie where are you!" Demon yelled coming into the room

" I'm showering give me a couple minutes " I said continuing to scrub myself before rinsing off and wrapped a towel around myself

I got dressed and hung my towel up and went into the room

" What did you need" I said getting in the bed and turning on my side my back facing him

" Nothing was just checking where you were" he said calmer than usual

Demon was so mean to me and he was nice and sweet to everyone else

It was like I was being punished for something that I didn't know about

" I will be right back" I said getting up and going into the bathroom and shutting it

I slid down the door and silently cried

I cry too easily

My face rested on top of my knees and I wiped my eyes inhaling and exhaling and tried to calm myself

Living like this isn't healthy, it's toxic being around someone who hates you

And I don't know why I try to please him by cleaning, cooking, washing doing everything in the house

It's becoming depressing

I stood up and brushed my nightgown off and washed my face and rubbed my nose

I looked at myself trying to prep myself and then left the bathroom as if nothing happen

I got back in the bed and turned back on my side my back facing him

I finally closed my eyes just to be pulled to his naked muscular chest

" Why are you crying angel" Demon said brushing my blond hair from my cheek

" I wasn't crying " I said clearing my throat

He hummed in response before speaking

" Your not a very good liar and I heard you cause you clearly don't know how to be very quiet " he said

" It's nothing just leave it alone " I said

" I'm not going to ask again"

" It's the way you treat me, your treat me like shit Demon and it unhealthy for me to sit here with a toxic person, I'm the only person you treat so horribly everyone else around us you treat special and I love that for them but I have to live in darkness while you treat me like I'm worth nothing, I may not be doing much but taking care of children takes a toll on your body expecially when you have been doing it for 6 years yet still I wash, cook, clean make sure everything is in order so you won't have to come home and starve or anything and what do I get in return just to be treated like shit and put up a act to seem like I'm happy abd I'm not I really am not" I said wiping my eyes which where leaking

He sighed and pulled me into a hug and I cried on his shoulder

My heart aches so much from all the betrayal and everything I went through

" I'm sorry for making you feel that way and I will try no I will do better to make you feel loved because I really do love you Natalie you are the mother of my children and believe it or not the love of my life" he said rubbing my head and kissing my forehead

My eyes started getting heavy from all the crying and they where hurting

I finally closed my eyes and let sleep take over me

I hope things would be different

Chapter 8

Natalie's POV2 weeks later4 am

Natalie and the twins outfits

" Hold mommy's hand " I said to the twins as we where about to board the jet with the others

They held my hand and we walked up until we where inside

Over the past couple of weeks my relationship with Demon had improved so her kept his promise

" You guys excited" Chrissy said

" We are grandma" they said and she took there hands bringing them to their seats

I buckled into my seat and demon board a few minutes later and took his seat beside me and buckled in

" Good morning this is your captain speaking we are about to take off and start of journey to Italy please be sure to fasten your seatbelts and stay seated until told otherwise" he said and the plane started moving

I stared outside as the plane ran fast on the runway and it took off into the air

" And we are now in the sir please feel free to move around but if possibly stay seated as unexpected turbulence can take place" he said before cutting off again

" What hotel are we going to"

" Sogaris Contemporary Hotel" Demon said and I nodded

I leaned on the window and started to close my eyes

" You know you can lean on me right" Demon said calmly

I leaned on his shoulder and closed my eyes hoping that sleep would take over fast

And it did cause I was out like light

8 hours later

" River, Rain wake up we here " I said shaking the twins

They groaned before waking up and I picked up Rain and Demon picked up River

We walked down the stairs as black SUVS where parked up for us with security

Some of the security's came for our bags and Demons parents and sister got in one of the SUVS

Our bags in one and then Demon, me and the kids in one

The driver pulled off and he drove off to the hotel

In 15 minutes we where there and all the tiredness that the kids once where was now gone

They where so excited and started running around and I smiled

Demon signed us in and we headed to our rooms

The room Demon got us had two bedrooms a suite and another room where the kids could stay

" Mommy let's go swimmm" the twins said

" Okay calm down let's get you guys changed first" I said taking them to their room

I took there swimsuits out and took Rain to change with me

" Mommy when will I get boobies like you" Rain questioned

" When your a teenager " I said smiling at her

Natalie's outfit

The twins swimwear's

" Daddy where ready" the twins said

I slipped on a short over my bikini bottom as I didn't feel comfortable walking around Demon

" Alright let's go" Demon said who was now changed into shorts and he was shirtless

I diverted my eyes form him and held Rivers hand and we walked down to the private beach

" You gonna wear a shorts in the water" Demon questioned raising his eyebrow

" No I will take it off once I get to the water" I said

Once we got to the beach the kids ran off into the water with Demon

I sat down and watched as they played

" You not coming in mama" River asked

" Yea I'm coming" I said before standing up and dusting the sand off me

I took my shorts off and walked towards the water and got in

The kids started splashing me and I laughed enjoying this

I spun around River and Rain and they laughed

" You think it's funny to splash mommy huh" I said kissing them

I enjoyed the rest of the time with them until they got tired

Demon picked them both up and I took my shorts up and their towels throwing it over them

While we where walking back ingot cat calls making me uncomfortable and Demon made me walk infront of him and cursed at anyone who looked my way

Once we got back into the room I showered the kids, made them eat and got them dressed for bed

Once they where finally down I went to shower

I stripped and got in the hot shower rubbing my aching shoulder

" Mind if I join you" Demon said not waiting for my response he stepped in

I stood their uncomfortably as I felt his stare

He rubbed my shoulder easing the pain I was feeling

" Your so beautiful" he said kissing my neck and shoulder before backing me up on the wall and lifting my leg

He stared at me before kissing me

I instantly kissed back my hand on his face and his free hand around my neck

The kiss was deepened, he gripped my ass fully picking me up

He slapped my ass making it shake

He pulled away and looked at my breasts

" Stop looking at them" I said embarrassed and putting my face in his neck

" They are beautiful, you don't gotta be embarrassed about shit" he said pecking my lips again

We actually showered this time and I wrapped my towel around me and demon wrapped his around his waist

We went back to our room and I moisturized my body with my Nivea and slowly rubbed my body and massaged my shoulder and breast

I slipped my silk underwear on and my then my nightgown before brushing my teeth and getting in the bed

Demon got in after me and I willingly this time cuddled up to him

I sighed and finally let sleep take over me

Day 1 is over with 5 more days to go

Chapter 9

Natalie's POVVacation day 2

Natalie and the twins swimwear

@NatalieThomasItaly

Its all about family

I walked on the beach holding the twins hands

Demon was walking behide us

" Can we go in the water again mommy " Rain said giving me puppy eyes

" Sure but don't go too deep loves" I said to them as they ran off

A large veiny arm wrapped around my waist and pulled my closer to his side

" You enjoying the vacation so far" Demon said kissing my forehead

" I am, it's calming " I said

He hummed in response

" Where are your parents and sister"

" They went out in the town" he said

" Oh that's nice"

" Mommy, daddy come in the water" River yelled

" We good right here love" I said

Demon chuckled and threw me over his shoulder and ran in the water throwing me in

" Oh my fucking god!" I yelled

" Mommy said a bad word" Rain said covering her mouth

" I'm sorry it just slipped" I muttered

We started playing with the kids, dunking them in the water and just enjoying time as a family

Soon we got out and Demon wrapped a towel around my waist

I raised my eyebrow at him

" Don't need nobody looking at your ass" he said and I shook my head

I picked River up and he had Rain around his neck

We walked back to our room and I swiped our card before walking in

I changed the kids off and Demon left to go do something

•••••••

I was showering when I heard a loud bang coming from the living room and the kids screaming

I got out and wrapped a towel around me and the bathroom door was yanked opened

Men dressed in black shits and face covered with a black mask yanked me and pulled me into the room and shoved me on the bed

" Where's Demon "

" Where the hell are my children" I yelled

" If you don't talk now they will die"

" I don't fucking know where he is okay, he left an hour ago I swear" I said tears streaming from my eyes

" Is that so" he said stroking and pulled my hair before ripping my towel off

" Oh god please no leave me alone!" I yelled as he took his clothes off signaling the rest of the guys to leave

I screamed and yelled as he held me down

God he's going to rape me

He's going to rape me

I kicked and slapped but he pointed s gun at me

" Shut the fuck up and take it" He said

Tears streamed from my eyes as he started to force himself in me

" You tight as fuck"

Gun shots rang out in the hotel room and he placed his hands on my mouth putting his clothes back on and left me naked

" Don't make a sound"

All I could do was cry

The door was opened and a body dropped and Demon stood there with a gun and a toothpick in his mouth

" Gaston pleasant surprise what you doing to my wife and kids" Demon said the gun pointed at the guy

" Just getting a lil taste, you got you a tight lil mama"

" Mmm I see, get out" he said harshly and Gaston walked out and right as he hit the door he was shot in the head

" Fucking fool, you okay mama" Demon said rushing over to me

" Where are the kids" I said crying

" My mom just came for them" he said

I completely broke down and I hugged him forgetting I was naked

" What did he do, did he touch you" he said and I nodded

" He almost raped me" I said sniffling

" Hey listen nobody go hurt you ight, I don't know what clicked in that's fucking fools head" he muttered picking me up

I wrapped my legs around him and my arms around his neck

Demon through a towel over me and comforted me

" You want me to run you a bath" he asked and I nodded

He placed me on the bed and I wrapped myself properly in the towel

Demon left to the bathroom and water was heard running

Demon came back and I got up

I dropped my towel and got in the bath pulling my knees to my chest

" Hey listen it's okay, I promise I ain't go leave you and the kids by yourself ever again okay"

I just nodded and looked away

It was his fault I was almost raped, those people came here looking for him after all

I got out and wrapped a towel around me and walked out in silence

I slipped my underwear on, some pj's pants and shirt and got in the bed

" The kids are staying with my mom tonight" Demon said and I just nodded

I crawled in bed and cuddled under the blanket

Demon sighed and got in bed with me

I gave in and cuddled up to him

I just felt safe and comforted when I'm close to him

I finally drifted off to sleep

Will be safe here in Italy at all now

Chapter 10

Natalie's POV

The twins swimwear

" Mama please come to the pool with us" the twins begged

" Okay fine I will come" I said getting out of the bed

I really didn't have the energy as I was still feeling down but anything to make my babies happy

The smiled happily and left the room

I took my swimsuit out and a bucket hat out

I stripped and slipped the underwear part on

" You ready" Demon said

I nodded slipping the top of my bikini out

Natalie outfit

I sighed and pulled my hat on

" Hey Nat talk to me" Demon said holding my hand

" It feels like someone is touching me even when no one is touching me I can't even look at myself the same anymore Demon because of it, I couldn't even protect our children" I said sniffling

" It wasn't your fault, it was my fault I wasn't here to defend my family the way I was suppose to stop blaming yourself" he said pulling me into his chest and kissed my forehead and pecked my lips

He deepened the kiss and gropped my ass before pulling away hearing the kids footsteps

" You ready mama" Rain said poking her head through the door

" I am let's go" I said holding both there hands and we walked out if our new hotel room

Since the incident, Demon got a new room and hand security posted outside

We walked down the path, Demon behide us

Once the kids saw the water they sprinted towards in

I sat in the chair crossing my legs as men where giving me looks that made me uncomfortable

" They looking at that fat coochie printing " Tina said putting a towel over me

" Thank you " I said and she nodded

I leaned on her shoulder rested my head on her

" You feeling better"

I shrugged

" I'm holding on, I really just miss my sister " I said sniffling and she nodded rubbing my back

My sister was banned from ever talking to me and I haven't seen or spoken to her for 6 years

My parents said I was a bad influence for getting pregnant and didn't want her around me

" Hey what if I made Demon help you find her" Tina said

" Really" I said

" Yea I can get him to do it and hopefully while where here we can find her and she can come here " Tina said

" That would be great honestly " I said smiling

Chapter 11

Natalie's POV

"We're you going?" Demon asked as I fixed my hair

"Tina taking me out" I said

Natalie's outfit

Demon nuzzled his nose in my neck inhaling and exhaling

"You smell good"

"Thank you"

"You gotta go tonight," he said feeling on my chest

"Stop, and yes I gotta go," I said

"You go give me some when you get back"

"Some of what?" I said standing up and putting my phone and cards in my bag with some lip gloss

"Pussy" he said lighting a blunt

My eyes widened and like Jesus sent an angel a knock was heard

I quickly looked through the door and opened it for Tina

"Hey sister-in-law," Tina said hugging me

"Hey Tina" I said hugging her back

"Well let's go we have dinner reservations"

"Tina give us a second"

Tina nodded and left

"Take this," he said handing me a card

"Demon I don't need this"

"I wasn't asking," he said gripping my jaw

I nodded, and he pecked my lips and my forehead

" Alright go have fun," he said slapping my ass as I walked through the door
•••• " Sooo I'm pregnant," Tina said

"Oh my god I'm so happy for you," I said hugging her

"Your the first to know other than Edwin but I wanna make sure everything runs smoothly," she said

"So what's up with you and my brother"

"I don't know right now I guess we are taking it slow," I said

"Here's your food ladies"

We thanked the guy and duh into our baked macaroni and cheese with steak and asparagus

"This is good honestly," Tina said

"It is, gotta bring the kids here"

•••••

Ominous POV|Mature Content

Natalie walked into the bedroom in which she shared with Demon

The room was silent as she slipped her shoes and clothes off

The lights switched on scaring Natalie

"Gosh Demon you scared me," she said holding her chest

He just stood there looking at her naked body

She was also trapped in a trance staring at the naked man who stood in front of her

He softly gripped her neck and tongued her tongue drawing her to the edge

She couldn't resist him and he couldn't

They couldn't resist anymore; the desire was palpable between them. She lay on top of him; her soft, nude body pressing into his. They moved together, skin slapping and slipping against each other in their fervent movements. She could feel his powerful hands gripping her hips, rough and demanding. His breath against her neck was hot, his lips trailing down as they sunk deeper and deeper into their passionate embrace.

He flipped her over, and she grabbed onto his back as he began thrusting hard into her. He growled against her neck, his passion and intensity driving her wild. She clung onto him, her moans getting louder and louder with every movement. It was like a drug to both of them, the pleasure radiating through every muscle. I moved faster and faster, her body trembling with pleasure.

The pleasure built and built until it exploded, coming over them in waves. They cried out together, a perfect harmony of pleasure. They held each other tightly, their breath coming in ragged heaves.

Finally, they collapsed in a mess of sweaty limbs, slowly coming back down to reality. They stayed like that for a while, kissed and caressed until they both felt completely content. They drifted off, their minds and bodies still reeling in ecstasy.

Chapter 12

Natalie's POV

Natalie and the kids outfit

We where currently on our way home from our vacation

The kids where asleep as Demon drove

It was currently 1 am as I scrolled on Instagram looking at my recent post

@NatalieThomas

Swipe

Swipe

Little vacation dump with the family @fan- who's the guy?@fan- is that the kids father?@hater- finding a new baby daddy

" You hungry?"

" Not really, still kinda full from the food we had on the plane " I said turning my phone off

He hummed in response and rested his arm on my thigh••••

I picked up Rain and River and Demon carried the bags in

I laid them in there beds and covered them and kissed there foreheads

Turning there lights off I left and went to to our bedroom

Demon was laying on the bed with one of his hand over his eyes

I took some pj's out and sat on the bed removing my shoes and dress

A kiss was felt on my shoulder and Demon nuzzled his face in my neck

" Sleep like this tonight" he said caressing my naked chest

" Nope cause the kids might come in here "

" Mmm whatever " he mumbled pulling me on top of him

" Your so beautiful, everything about you is beautiful " he said caressing my cheek and rubbed my butt

" Thank you" I said kissing his fingers

" I wanna put these inside you"

" Stop" I said closing my legs as his fingers started rubbing my vagina through my underwear

He groaned burying his face in my neck

Gave this dude pussy twice and he hooked

" Lemme get dressed" I said trying to get up as he held me tightly

Mature Content

Demon shifted my underwear to the side before wetting his fingers with my juices

Sliding in two of his fingers I moaned stuffing my face in his neck as my face and neck got hot

" Getting shy on me baby," he said slapping my ass as he fingered me

I moaned loudly in the crook of his neck as his fingers curved in me

" Ride my fingers Mama or I will stop," he said kissing my neck

I moaned as I slid up and down on his long fingers, My hand rested on his chest as I rode his fingers

Suddenly I felt empty as I was nearing my climax

"Why would you d-" I gasped as his thick dick filled me up

" Oh fuck" I mumbled biting my lips as he slapped and gripped my ass and started to pound into me

" Demonnnn fuck " I yelled as he slammed into me repeatedly

" Ride your dick baby," he said slapping my ass and gripping my jaw making me stare right into his eyes my mouth opened wide as I slid his dick me

I gripped his shoulders as I rode his dick my ass clapping and my breast bouncing from the action

" Oh fuck yes " I yelled loudly as my eyes crossed while I painted his dick with my cream

I was shaking as he kept slamming into me going deeper into me

" Fuck " he groaned his deep voice vibrating in my neck as he cummed in me

I slid him out of me before going on my knees and tapped his dick on my tongue

I sucked on the tip licking it as he groaned looking at me

I bopped my head as I stroked what could not fit in my mouth and rubbed his balls with my neck

He gripped my hair roughly as he pushed my head further on his dick letting me get air after a few seconds

I moaned softly before he pulled me up and we got in the 69 position

He buried his face deep in my pussy as I buried his dick deep in my throat

He gripped my ass and squeezed it as he ate me out making me moan

Realizing he was near I quickly spun around and started riding him again rocking back and forth my placing my hands on either side of his head and slamming down on his dick making me yell out and he let out a deep moan

Continuing to ride him he gripped my hips and slammed me down before he cummed in me

End of Mature Content

I breathed heavily as I slid his dick from inside me and laid on his chest

" Fuck girl you definitely not going nowhere," he said rubbing my ass cheek

A couple minutes went by and we soon fell asleep

Chapter 13

Natalie's POV

Natalie and the kids' outfit

I watched as my children ran around in the backyard, Their tutor just left and I wanted to give them some play time before dinner which was baked Ziti

The demon was out for work as usual and I had no idea what time he would be back usual

" Alright come on kids wash up I'm gonna make dinner?" I said

They ran inside and I closed the doors entering the kitchen

Taking out the ingredients I needed I started to make dinner

While multitasking I made some iced tea dropping ice cubes in the jug

....

I made the children's plate and poured their drink out as they sat patiently at the table

" Mommy when is daddy coming home?" Rain asked

" I don't know hun he didn't say" I responded having my own dinner

They sighed and their face turned into a pout as they ate

Once they were done they helped me clean up before moving to their bedroom to watch a movie

I sat on the couch watching a lifetime movie while my phone rested on my lap

After a few minutes, I powered the TV off and went to the bedroom

Taking some clothes from my side of the closet I went to the bathroom and stripped while the water heated up

" I think older just a little bit older" I sang as my playlist started playing

I stood in the shower as the water ran down my once dry body making it wet

Using my strawberry Pound Cake bodywash I poured some on my wash cloth and lathered my body making sure to rub underneath my breast and get my back

Rinising the wash cloth out I used my Yoni soap before washing my lady areas and butt and then wash the cloth out putting it back in its respectful area

I washed my body off then added my body scrub then washed off again

Turning the shower off I wrapped myself in my fluffy black towel and dried my skin

Moizturing my body with my coconut oil I slipped on my lace underwear and a dress

Tieing the front of my dress I started combing my hair and placed it in a highbun before doing my skincare

Adding on lip balm I checked the time

It was 8pm

" kids!" I called out going into their bedroom

" yes mama" they answered

" time for bed"

" but we want to wait for daddy to get home mommy" River said pouting

" I know my loves but daddy is running a bit late" I said ruffling their hairs

" have you brushed your teeth?" I questioned

They nodded showing my their teeth

" Good job now lemme tuck you in"

Putting them both in their beds I covered their bodys and kissed their foreheads before reading them bible story of Jonah

Once they were asleep I stood up

" Good night my little loves" I said kissing them again before turning there lights off

Leaving there door ajar I went back to my bedroom

getting into bed I turned the TV on and watched Nowhere on Netflix

Few minutes pasted and the bedroom door opened and Demon walked in loosing his tie

" The kids were waiting for you" I spoke in the dark

" I had to work later than usual"

" Mhm sure, your dinner is downstairs" I replied continuing my dinner

He sighed before getting in bed and laying his head on my breast and his hand wrapped protectively around my waist

I rubbed his back my acrylic connecting with his bare skin

Soon small snores were heard and he was out like light

Fast asleep comfortably as his face was stuffed into my breast and a small droll leaving his mouth

Maybe today was a busy day as he had implied

I maybe am just overthinking

But if I was wasn't

I stared at him envisioning him fucking another female a the urge to slap him the face and say it wasn't me was their

" I didn't cheat relax" he muttered in his sleep rubbing my butt

I hummed in responce and continued watching my movie

Chapter 14

Natalie's POV

Natalie's outfit

" Love!" Demon called out

" I'm in the kitchen " I said

His heavy footsteps were heard as he entered the kitchen

Hugging me from behind I leaned into his embrace

" I have a surprise for you"

I smiled turning around

" And what would that be" I said as he covered my eyes

" You will have to wait and see"

As we walked through the house my feet connected with warm pavement if our backyard

What could possibly be outside

" You ready?"

I nodded excitedly

Tears filled my eyes as I saw what stood in front of me

" Oh my god "

I cried running into the embrace of my younger sister who was now much taller than me

" Your so beautiful Delilah"

Delilah

" Demon reached out to me and I didn't hesitate to contact him back I missed you so much " she said tears streaming down her face

" Oh were such cry babies like old time" I said as we laughed together

Demon watched from afar a small smile before it disappeared

" So how's life what's been happening"

" Well I'm now married,two beautiful children"

I teared up, I missed everything that happened in my sister's life

" I'm so proud of you "

" What about you? What's happening where's is your baby?"

" Well I have two kids also turns out they were twins, they are upstairs having there tutor session and we'll I'm not married like I would have hoped"

" So you and demon aren't married?"

" No uh it's complicated, he just learnt about his kids a year ago basically and well we're working from there I guess" I said shrugging

She nodded understandable

" How's mom and dad?"

She sighed

" Well dad died a year after you left in a car crash and mom is suffering from stage 4 bone cancer"

I gasped, even though my parents had wronged me I loved them dearly

" She regrets kicking your out, she says it was all dad's doing because he didn't want to ruin his image" Delilah said

" I want to see her, I want the kids to meet her atleast "

" We moved from here as soon as you left, we now live in New York"

" That's why the house was burnt down" I said sadly

My father really didn't want me finding them again

She nodded rubbing my shoulders

" I will talk to Demon about it, I'm sure he will book us a flight to New York " I said and she nodded

" Mommyyy!" Rain yelled coming downstairs her hair in dismay

" Rain what have you been up to?"

" That lady is stressful" she said tiredly dropping onto my lap

" You left your brother ?"

"More like he left me bed fast asleep " she said frowning

" Who's this mommy she looks like you"

Delilah smiled

" This is my you get sister Deliliah also known as your aunty "

" Is she the one you use to tell us stories about"

I nodded, Rain smiled hugging Deliliah who hugged her back instantly tearing up

" She's perfect" Delilah said her lips trembling as she rubbed Rains hair

Demon soon came downstairs with a tired River

" Might have to hire a new tutor " Demon said after pecking my lips

" Who's that mommy?"

" That's your Aunty Deliliah the one I always tell you stories about"

He smiled excitedly joining the grow hug

" They are perfect" Delilah said

I had hidden my pregnancy for 2 months from my parents and Delilah was the only one who knew about it, everyday she would play with my small bump kissing it and talking to them

She was only 15 at the time and our bond was perfect we did everything together

" Can I talk to you"

Demon and I left to the kitchen

" I want to go to New York with the kids, my mom has stage 4 bone cancer and I would like to see her one last time"

" Why would you want to see such a horrible person" Demon frowned

" It wasn't her doing but my father's who is now deceased "

Demon sighed rubbing his face

"I will get you all on flight by tomorrow but you will return the day after in the night"

" Can't I stay a week?"

" Fine"

As the time became later i showed Delilah her room and got her some clothes that may fit her since she was in the slimmer side

" You good in here?"

" Yeah I'm good"

I nodded hugging her before leaving the room

I went to our bedroom where Demon was standing on his phone butt ass naked

" Demon!" I squealed covering my eyes

" Relax you have seen me naked before" he said chuckling

" Yeah when were having sex "

" C'mere"

Demon pulled me in between his legs and I refused to look down at the Demon between his legs

" These pants look uncomfortable* he said smirking looking at me as he tugged it down revealing my lace thong that barely covered my coochie

" Were not having sex tonight, because everytime you cum in me and refuse to buy me plan b" I said frowning and crossing my arm

" We haven't fucked in 2 weeks "

" And your still alive aren't you" I said pulling the isn't off completely before walking to my side of the closet

Demon groaned dropping back on the bed

I took my sleeping shorts out with my top and took his dick in my hand stroking it before getting dressed

I took my top off and my tender breast bounced about, my period seemed to be coming

" Listen if I hold your ass it's over remember that shit " he said stroking his hard dick

Demon grabbed me pushing me in my knees and holding my hair forcing me to watch him jerk off

He knew he had control over my body

He moaned looking in my eyes as I bit my lips feeling myself get wet

His cum spilled on my face and he groaned slapping it against my face

I sucked the tip off which bad cum remaining as he jerked forward

" You my freak guh" he said kissing me passionately

He's my Demon

Chapter 15

N atalie's POV

Natalie's outfit

Twins outfit

" Bye daddy" Rain said hugging her dad after River

" Be good and when you get back I will take you to Maldives" Demon said

He spoils them so bad

They nodded rubbing off with there aunt inside the private jet

" I love you, stay safe"

" I love you too" I replied softly my arms around his neck

He captured my lips with his before kissing my forehead

" Call me when you land so I can send a driver"

" It's okay Demon, Deliliah's husband will be getting us " I said and he sighed nodding

" Alright run along "

" Bye " I said hugging him again before walking away

Once I entered the jet door closed and I got in my seat

" It is so great to meet you" Alexander my sister's husband said

" An honor to meet you as well" I said

We had just made it outside the airport and we're now getting ready to go see my mommy

" She is actually a bit happy today so you came on a perfect day"

I nodded holding the twins close to me

The drive wasn't long it was about 10 minutes

The house was a farm like style home and it was beautiful

" You guys go in and I will bring the bags "

" Mom I have a surprise for you " Delilah said

" What may that be "

My mother was now fully grey with her glasses on and knitting as usual, smiling it warmed my heart

" Mommy" I said stepping in the room

She gasped her pale wrinkled arms shaking

" Natalie"

She sobbed as I got in my knees to hug her

" Oh my beautiful girl "

" Look at you all fabulous and healthy, weres the baby oh don't tell me you left the child behind"

" I didn't and it's actually children I had twins" I said and she broke down

" I'm so sorry, my baby I'm so sorry "

River and Rain entered the room with Deliliah

" Mom this are your grandchildren, River and Rain"

" You named them after my parents "

I nodded

She hugged them tightly

" I'm your Nana my dears, oh she resembles you so much but the boy I assume he looks like his father"

I nodded

" He does, there father couldn't make it but you will meet him " I said

" These are my babies" Delilah said entering with a cubby baby boy and a little toddler by her side

" Oh my there's so precious, I'm your aunty Natalie " I said lowering down rhe little toddlers side

She pulled me into a hug with her tiny arms causing me to sob

After 6 years I was back with my father even though I missed out on so much

" Where did you get a baby" Demon said in the FaceTime

" This is my nephew Nathaniel" I said bouncing the baby boy in my arms

" He's precious isn't he, I want one " I said pouting

Demon stares at me as those words leave my mouth

" Not right now atleast " I said clearing my throat while Demon chuckled

" Mmm we will talk when you get back home if your not already pregnant"

" Demon please" I said

Nathaniel cuddled into my breast sticking his hand in my bra

" Your a brave one " Demon said side eyeing the child

" Leave him be " I said laughing

" He's found his new victim " Deliliah said

" He tends to do it a lot with females he is comfortable with, he's a bit cheeky" she said and I chuckled

I smiled as she snapped a photo of us

" A fresh photo for the photo album "

" I will call you later love when the kids are going to bed "

" Okay be safe "

"Always"

" So much for not dating "

" As I said it's complicated " I said smiling

" Mhm as long as your happy "

It felt so good to be back with my family after being apart for so long

Chapter 16

Natalie's POV

Natalie's outfit

" You okay love " Demon asked concerned

" Yeah just not feeling too good in my stomach probably some stuff I ate back in New York"

He nodded pulling me close as we laid in bed together

" You just started feeling ill?"

" Since we got back last week, threw up everything I ate " I said

" Gonna get somebody to come check you?"

Opening my phone I checked my phone seeing that my period was late by 2 weeks

I sat up straight and Demon looked over at my phone

" Your periods late?"

" Yeah it was supposed to be here from last week" I said getting up and going to the bathroom

Demon watched me closely as I tore down the drawers

Finally finding two unopending box of pregnancy test Demon looked at me

" Fuck " he mumbled

" You don't think it's possible right"

" Natalie of course it possible we been fucking raw"

Nervously opening the boxes I peed in the test leaving them to load

" Relax your shaking " Demon said rubbing my shoulders

" Really Demon relax? Our relationship isn't even stable enough for our two children but to have three?"

" We are in a stable enough relationship Natalie, the fuck you mean?"

" Were basically just fucking fuck buddy's Demon we haven't made anything official at all " I explained

" Natalie then what else would we be huh?!"

" Unless your seeing somebody else that I don't fucking know about " he yelled making me jump

My phone alarm went off and I shakily looked at the test

Positive written over both indicating that I was 4 weeks pregnant

" Oh god" I said holding my head

Demon has already left the bathroom before I told him the results

Tears welled in my eyes, picking up my phone I called Demon who's phone rang in th bedroom indicating that he left it there

It was now 4 am in the morning and Demon had yet to return

The bed dipped and large tattooed arm was wrapped around my waist and rested onto my stomach

" Im sorry, we go get through it okay "

I nodded resting my hand on top of his

10Am

" Come eat kids" I said

They ran downstairs and my phone rang

Delilah's contact popped up and I answered

" Hello sister"

" Helloooo,how's mom this morning " I said smiling

" She's good, she having breakfast with Navi "

I nodded

" I'm pregnant again " I said

She squealed

" Oh my god I'm so happy for you guys when did you find out?"

" Last night "

" You don't seem too happy "

" I am, it's just I wasn't really ready to expand the family but I wasn't having protected sex either so "

" Demon wouldn't leave you for the world you two will figure out "

I nodded

" Did you book your first appointment?"

" Demon booked one for at home tomorrow so I will see what's up, I will tell mommy everything after the doctor confirms " I said

" Okay "

" Yeah, how are the kids though?"

" There good they miss you dearly "

I smiled

" I miss them too, you guys should come see us next month "

" We will try and see, gotta see how work is going to look"

I nodded

" Mommy daddy is back "

Demon walked in to were I was removing his shoes and jacket leaving him in a muscle tee and sweatpants

I muted my microphone

" Where did you go?"

" Went for a run" he said

" Mmm"

Looking away from him I unmuted my mic

" Im gonna call you later sis "

" Alright bye " I said

I hung up the call and sighed heavily

" Still thinking?"

" Well am I supposed to stop"

He gave me a hard look before walking away

I probably should stop giving him such a hard time

I leaned my head against my arm and thought back to everything that has happened

Since Demon came back into my life it changed for good

Now that I was possibly be pregnant again it would be easier since he was around

I should accept it and move on

This is just another blessing that came in not such a very well time